HILLTOP ELEMENTARY SCHOOL

The Snowman

RAYMOND BRIGGS

RANDOM HOUSE NEW YORK

Library of Congress Cataloging-in-Publication Data:
Briggs, Raymond. The snowman. SUMMARY: When his snowman comes to
life, a little boy invites him home and in return is taken on a flight
above beautiful cities and strange lands.
[1. Stories without words. 2. Dreams—Fiction] I. Title PZ7.B7646Sn [E] 78-55904
ISBN: 0-394-83973-0 (hardcover); 0-394-88466-3 (pbk.); 0-394-93973-5 (lib. bdg.)

Manufactured in the United States of America   20 19 18 17

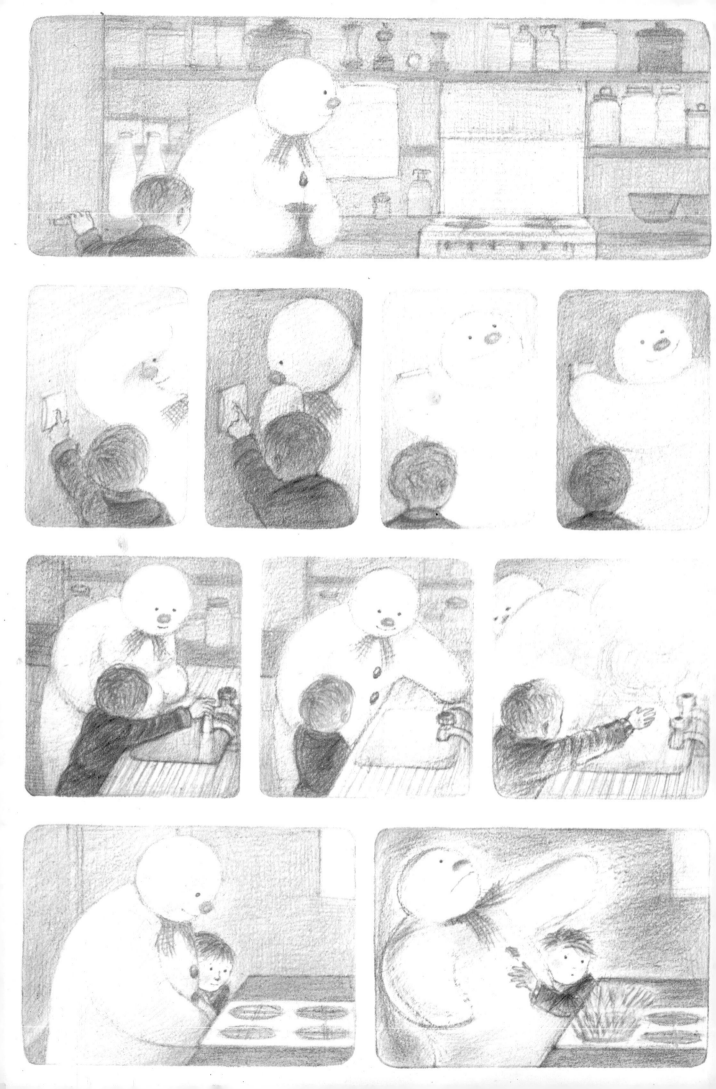

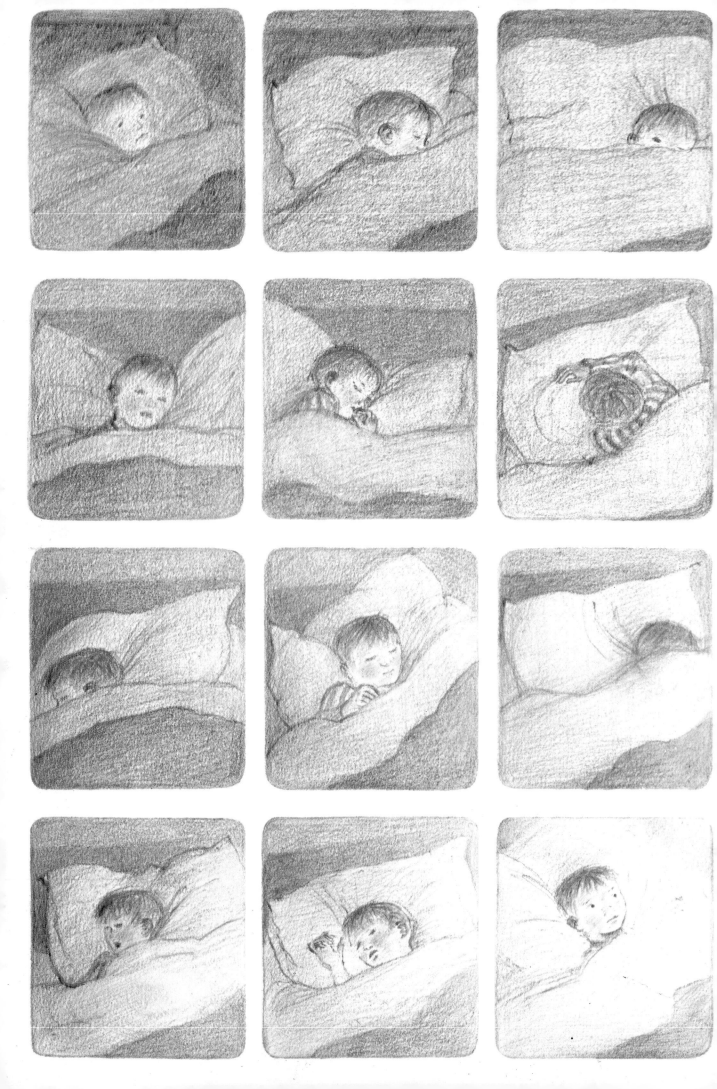